TEN LITTLE EGGS

A Celebration of Family

Illustrated by Jess Mikhail

ZONDERkidz

One cracked open and what did Mama see?

A soft, tiny bluebird singing sweetly as can be.

One cracked open and what did Mama see?

A golden, brown eaglet looking brave as can be.

One cracked open and what did Mama see?

A bright, pink flamingo with legs long as can be.

One cracked open and what did Mama see?

A rainbow-billed toucan just as colorful as can be.

SIX little eggs in a nest in a tree.

One cracked open and what did Mama see?

A slimy baby turtle perched UP IN A TREE?

FIVE little eggs in a nest in a tree.

One cracked open and what did Mama see?
A funny baby platypus, confused as can be.

One cracked open and what did Mama see?

A teeny, tiny hummingbird buzzing like a bumblebee.

THREE little eggs in a nest in a tree.

One cracked open and what did Mama see?

A fuzzy little penguin walking wobbly as can be.

One cracked open and what did Mama see?

A sparkly little goldfish blowing bubbles from the sea.

One cracked open and what did Mama see?
An alligator grinning ...

Is he going to eat me????

Looks like somebody needs a hug!

TEN little babies
in a nest in a tree.

All my little loved ones— my new family.

Each little baby, all snuggled up tight, under Mama's wings and ready for GOOD NIGHT.